The Grinning Gargoyle Mystery

The Bobbsey Twins®

The Grinning Gargoyle Mystery

Laura Lee Hope

Illustrated by Rudy Nappi

WANDERER BOOKS
Published by
Simon & Schuster, Inc, New York

Copyright © 1986 by Simon & Schuster, Inc.
All rights reserved
including the right of reproduction
in whole or in part in any form
Published by WANDERER BOOKS
A Division of Simon & Schuster, Inc.
Simon & Schuster Building
1230 Avenue of the Americas
New York, New York 10020

THE BOBBSEY TWINS, WANDERER and colophon are registered
trademarks of Simon & Schuster, Inc.

Manufactured in the United States of America
10 9 8 7 6 5 4 3 2 1

Library of Congress Cataloging in Publication Data
ISBN: 0-671-62333-8
Hope, Laura Lee.
The grinning gargoyle mystery.

(The Bobbsey twins; 14)
Summary: The Bobbsey twins are drawn into a mystery
involving the manufacture of perfume while on a family
vacation in Paris.
[1. Mystery and detective stories] I. Nappi, Rudy,
ill. II. Title. III. Series: Hope, Laura Lee.
Bobbsey twins (1980–   ); 14.
PZ7.H772Gr   1986   [Fic]   86-5632
ISBN 0-671-62333-8 (pbk.)

Contents

. 1 .

An Urgent Call

"There's a flash!" cried six-year-old Freddie Bobbsey, squinting at the burst of light over the treetops.

"Long or short?" asked his big sister Nan.

"Long—and now there's a little quick one!"

"Dash-dot . . . that's the letter N," said Nan, writing it down.

The Bobbsey twins were having fun, signaling back and forth with mirrors between their home and the lumberyard Mr.

Bobbsey owned. They were using mirrors to reflect the bright summer sunshine. Nan's twin, Bert, had read that soldiers used to signal to each other this way before there were radios or telephones.

More flashes of light glinted in the distance until the message read: NAN HURRY HOME.

"I wonder if anything's wrong?" Freddie blurted out.

"Dunno, the message isn't over yet. Keep watching!" Nan urged. "There's another short flash!"

"And another one—and another! That makes three dots," Freddie counted.

"Dot-dot-dot is S in Morse code."

Dark-haired, twelve-year-old Nan and her blond younger brother were up in the little cupola, or tower, on top of their dad's warehouse and office. Their twins, Bert and Flossie, were at the Bobbseys' attic window.

Their house was in a hilly part of Lake-

8

port, higher up than the part of town near the waterfront where the lumberyard was located. So it was easy to see the sun flashes over the roofs and treetops.

Soon Nan had copied down the rest of the message. It read: SOMETHING CAME FROM FRANCE.

"Hey, I'll bet it's from Miss Palmer!" Freddie exclaimed.

"I bet so, too," Nan agreed happily.

Julie Palmer had been a general science teacher at the Lakeport School. She was one of Nan's favorite teachers, as well as a good friend. A year before, Miss Palmer had left the school to become a laboratory chemist and later went to France, but she and Nan still corresponded.

"Come on, let's go home and read her letter!" said Nan, picking up her hand mirror.

"Just a letter?" Freddie sounded disappointed as they started down the tower stairs.

"What's wrong with a letter?"

"Bert wouldn't tell you to hurry home just for a measly little letter, would he?"

"Why not? It's probably something about meeting us after we get to Paris."

The Bobbsey family was planning to fly to France for a long-awaited summer vacation. Their first stop would be the beautiful city of Paris, and Nan had already written her teacher friend to tell her when they expected to arrive.

"I'll bet it's something more than just a letter," Freddie persisted as the two children came scampering out into the lumberyard.

"We'll see!"

A big, husky black man was loading fence posts and planks of wood into the back of a red pickup truck.

"Looks like Sam's going to make a delivery," said Freddie. "Maybe he'll give us a lift home."

"Good idea." As they turned toward the

pickup, Nan called out, "Any chance you'll be going by the house, Sam?"

"Sure will. Want a ride?"

"Oh, yes—if it won't be out of your way?"

"Not at all—hop in! In fact, you can do me a favor. Tell Dinah I promised to dig some postholes for Mrs. Thursby over in Shorewood, so I may be a bit late getting home to supper."

"Better not be *too* late, 'cause she's making fried chicken and cherry pie."

Sam Johnson chuckled as he hoisted Nan's little brother up into the cab of the truck. "Don't you worry about me—Dinah knows I'll be expecting a double helping!"

Sam was married to the family's cook and housekeeper, Dinah Johnson. The couple lived on the top floor of the Bobbseys' house.

With the truck all loaded and the two children beside him, he drove away from the lumberyard.

"Thanks! . . . Thanks a lot, Sam!" they said as they climbed down from the truck minutes later.

"Take care now!" Sam grinned and waved before driving off.

Flossie had seen them from the window and came running out of the house, her golden curls swinging and bobbing. "Nan! Nan! Wait'll you see what the mailman brought you!"

She held out a package in one chubby little hand. The package wasn't very big, just about the size of a tape cassette, and bore several French postage stamps. There was also a green tag, showing it had been checked and okayed by the U.S. Customs Service.

"See! I told you it wasn't just a letter!" crowed Freddie. "Who's it from?"

"Miss Palmer!" said Nan as she saw the writing on the label. "We were both right about that!"

They hurried inside and were met by Bert in the living room. "What do you

12

suppose it is, Nan?" He looked as eager and curious as the younger twins.

"Search me—give me a chance to open it first!"

Inside the heavy wrapping was a box which contained a pretty little green-glass bottle. Its tiny stopper was sealed with wax.

"Ooh, maybe it's perfume!" gasped Flossie.

Nan's brown eyes sparkled with anticipation, and she began picking off the wax with her fingernails. "Something tells me you're a good guesser!"

"Wait, look!" her little sister exclaimed. "There's a note in the box, too!"

Flossie plucked out a card and handed it to Nan, who took time to read what it said aloud:

" '*Wish me luck, Nan dear! I'll tell you all about it when you get to Paris.*' And it's signed '*Julie P.*' "

"What does she mean, 'Wish me luck'?" Freddie puzzled.

"Don't ask me!" Nan finished scraping off the wax and pulled out the tiny glass stopper. Then she held the bottle up to her nose.

"Mm-m-m-m, it *is* perfume!" she announced. "And it's absolutely *heavenly!*"

"Let me smell!"—"No, let me!" the little twins clamored.

Nan let them take turns sniffing the fragrance. Freddie reported to Bert that it smelled "okay," but Flossie reacted as ecstatically as her big sister.

"I remember now, back in kindergarten," she exclaimed, "whenever Miss Palmer had hall duty, she always had beautiful-smelling perfume on!"

Nan smiled. "Yes, and her science room always smelled nice, too, because she kept it full of lovely flowers!"

"Flowers are what perfume's made from, isn't it?" said Bert after he, too, had inhaled the fragrance.

Nan nodded. "Some perfume is floral—like the kind Mom wears. But they use

14

spices and lots of other things, too, in making . . ."

The dark-haired Bobbsey girl broke off as she suddenly picked up on what her twin was thinking. "Gosh, maybe you're right, Bert! Maybe Miss Palmer made up this perfume herself in her own lab!"

Nan hurried into the kitchen to show her mother and Dinah what her former science teacher had sent her from Paris. Both admired the lovely scent.

"My stars!" breathed Dinah when Nan dabbed some on the housekeeper's wrist, the way she had seen salespeople do at perfume counters. "Sam'll really think I'm glamorous when he gets a whiff of *this!*"

"It's exquisite," Mrs. Bobbsey agreed. "If Julie Palmer can find a company to manufacture and sell her perfume, I think it could become very popular. I'll certainly encourage her to try when we see her in Paris."

The Bobbseys' vacation trip was less than a week away. Late one afternoon, several days after Nan received the package from France, the telephone rang. The younger twins were playing by themselves in the living room, so Flossie answered.

"This is Julie Palmer calling from Paris, dear," said a voice on the line.

Flossie's blue eyes grew big as saucers when she realized that the phone call was coming all the way across the Atlantic Ocean. "From P-P-Paris?!" she stuttered.

"Yes. You remember me, don't you, Flossie, from school? I'd like to speak to Nan."

The golden-haired little girl was so excited, the right words couldn't seem to find their way out of her mouth. Seeing his twin's excited look and hearing her mention Paris, Freddie stopped playing with his robot and rushed over to help her.

"Is this Miss Palmer?" he blurted, taking the phone boldly.

"That's right. You must be Freddie. Is your big sister there, Freddie?"

"No, ma'am, Nan's not home. But we'll be flying over to see you soon, Miss Palmer."

"I know, that's why I'm calling." The teacher hesitated. She sounded not only disappointed that she couldn't speak to Nan, but Freddie had a feeling that she was worried, too. "Would you give Nan a message for me, please?"

"Yes, ma'am."

"I assume she got that little bottle of perfume I sent her. Did she?"

"Oh, yes! She thought it smelled wonderful—and so did Flossie and Mom and Dinah!"

"I'm glad they liked it. Now listen, Freddie, will you please tell Nan to bring that little bottle of perfume with her when you come to Paris? I'll be waiting at the airport and explain everything when your flight gets in."

"Okay, I'll tell her, Miss Palmer."

"Good boy! And please don't forget,

Freddie! This is very, very urgent because
I . . ."

Julie Palmer's voice suddenly faded behind a crackle of static. The next thing
Freddie heard was the dial tone.

Somehow the telephone call from Paris
had been cut off!

. 2 .

Airport Adventure

Charles de Gaulle Airport, just outside of Paris, was named for a famous French general who became the President of France. The air terminal was bustling with people on the hot July day when the Bobbseys arrived there to start their vacation.

"Where's Miss Palmer?" said Flossie, looking all around.

"I don't see her anywhere," Bert said. "You sure she knew when our plane was due to land, Nan?"

"Of course I'm sure. I sent her all the details about our flight and what hotel we'd be staying at. She's probably here right now, somewhere in this crowd. We'll just have to be patient."

There were so many travelers and people on hand to see them off or to greet them, as well as skycaps pushing carts loaded with suitcases, that it would certainly not be hard, Nan thought, to miss someone you were looking for.

The Bobbseys had already collected their own luggage off the carousel and had it and their passports inspected by the French customs and immigration officers. Now all they could do was wait for Julie Palmer.

In a way, this was the hardest part of their trip so far, because they were all eager for their first sight of Paris. The little twins were squirming and fidgeting impatiently, and Mr. Bobbsey had just taken out his handkerchief for the second time to wipe the perspiration off his forehead.

"Maybe we should have her paged," he muttered to his wife. "What do you think, Mary?"

"As Nan says, we'll have to be patient. Let's give her a little longer, Dick." Suddenly Mrs. Bobbsey touched her husband's arm. "Wait . . . I wonder if this could be someone she sent to meet us?"

A thin man with a dark bushy mustache had just pushed his way through the crowd in the airport lounge. His eyes seemed to be sizing them up as he strode toward them.

"Pardon, madame, m'sieu," he said. "Are you perhaps the Bobbsey family?"

"That's right," said Mr. Bobbsey. "We're waiting for Julie Palmer."

"Ah, oui! Mam'zelle Palmer and I, we are friends. She sent me here to find you." His sharp eyes flickered over the two sets of twins and fastened on Nan. "And this young lady, I think, must be Miss Nan Bobbsey—*n'est-ce pas?*"

"That's right," Nan said, wondering what had happened to her friend.

"And you brought the perfume sample that Julie Palmer has sent you?" The man spoke with an accent that made her name sound like *Zhulie Palmaire.*

Nan nodded. "Yes, I have it right here." Reaching in her bag, she took out the pretty little green-glass bottle to show him.

"Ah, *c'est bon!* She sent me here to get it for her. This note—it will explain all."

The mustached man fished in his pocket and pulled out an envelope with Nan's name typed on it. Inside was a note, also typed:

Dear Nan,

I have been delayed but will get in touch with you later at your hotel.

In the meantime, please give the perfume to the man who brings you this note.

Julie

The man reached out for the little green bottle. But to everyone's surprise, Nan held it back out of his reach!

The man's face darkened in a scowl. "What is the matter?" he blurted gruffly. "Did you not read the note?"

"Yes, I read it . . . b-b-but I'm not sure it's from Julie," Nan said in a nervous voice. "So I'm not going to give you the perfume unless . . . unless we can talk to her on the telephone, or something like that!"

The man's mouth opened, then closed again. For a moment he didn't seem to know what to do or to say. Nan's refusal had evidently taken him by surprise.

Without warning, the stranger suddenly seized her by the arm and snatched the bottle out of her hand!

The others could hardly believe their eyes. Mr. Bobbsey was outraged and lunged forward angrily with one fist clenched. "Now just a minute, mister—!"

Bert was also ready to get physical, but the man darted away before either could lay a hand on him. He was heading for the nearest exit.

24

Freddie, however, who was nearest the mustached crook, moved fastest of all. He managed to catch hold of the thief's pantleg and hang on with all his might.

Even though the little boy was jerked off his foot, the action threw the fleeing man off balance. The man went sprawling head first! The perfume bottle flew from his grasp and went sliding across the floor of the air terminal!

Bert grabbed it before the thief could recover. With a snarl, the mustached man scrambled upright. He glared furiously at both Bobbsey boys but knew there was no chance of getting back the perfume without colliding head-on with a very angry Mr. Bobbsey. He dashed off and, in seconds, was out of sight among the airport crowd.

"Don't go after him, Dick!" begged Mrs. Bobbsey, holding onto her husband's arm anxiously. "It's not worth the risk of getting hurt."

Mr. Bobbsey fumed but controlled his temper. "You were a brave boy, Freddie, to

stop that fellow the way you did," he said, patting his small son on the shoulder.

"Oh yes, my hero! You're wonderful!" giggled Flossie. She hugged and kissed her twin, while Freddie made a face.

"And that was fast thinking on your part, Bert," his father added. "At least the sneak didn't get away with anything!"

Bert handed the little bottle to Nan, saying, "Hope it's okay."

"It is," she reported with relief, after checking the glass. "Not even cracked! Thanks a lot for saving it, you two!"

"But how did you ever guess the man was a crook?" her mother asked.

"Look how my name was spelled." Nan held out the envelope. It was addressed to NAN BOBSEY. "Miss Palmer would never make such a mistake! Besides, when she writes me, her letters are never typed— they're always in her own handwriting."

"Smart thinking, Nan," said Mr. Bobbsey. He started to pick up some of their luggage but stopped as he saw a woman hurrying toward them through the crowd.

The bystanders had gaped in surprise when the would-be thief fell and then fled. The whole incident, however, had lasted less than a minute and, by now, most of the spectators had lost interest.

But the young woman approaching the Bobbseys looked very much concerned over what had happened. She was wearing jeans and a knit top and had dark red hair.

"That man with the mustache, did he try to steal something from you, *chérie?*" she asked Nan.

"Yes, this little bottle of perfume."

The redhead's eyes glinted with interest. "Ah, *oui*—I am not surprised. He is a bad type, that fellow Lachine—a known thief and swindler, with several arrests on his record. I will report what happened to the airport police!"

Before the Bobbseys could ask her any questions, she turned and walked swiftly away.

. 3 .

Where Is Julie?

During the next fifteen minutes, Julie Palmer herself did not appear. Nor did anyone call back when Mr. Bobbsey asked a clerk at the airline counter to have her paged over the P.A. system.

"I guess there's no sense waiting any longer," Mrs. Bobbsey said with a sigh. Nan was disappointed, but the others were only too eager to start for their hotel.

Somehow the whole family, with luggage, managed to squeeze into a single taxi. The younger twins sat on their parents' laps, while Bert and Nan each clutched a flight bag.

When Paris at last came into full glorious view, it was everything that Nan had read about and longed to see. She loved the wide boulevards and chestnut trees and sidewalk cafes. The policemen in their capes and uniforms, and young people dressed in far-out fashions looked just the way she had seen them in photographs and movies. And most of all, she loved the River Seine, winding its way through the heart of Paris, with picturesque arching bridges and a glimpse of Notre Dame Cathedral in the distance.

"Oh, I can hardly wait to explore Paris!" she murmured, half to herself.

"That's exactly what we'll do this afternoon, honey," Mr. Bobbsey promised.

The travel agency had booked them into a modest family hotel in the Latin Quarter. As they lunched at a nearby restaurant that Mrs. Bobbsey had picked out, they chattered away about which of the city's famous sights they should see first.

"Why not just play it by ear and enjoy ourselves?" said Bert.

"Sounds like the best idea so far," his dad chuckled. "All in favor say 'Aye.'"

Everyone laughed and chorused *Aye!*

"Just think of all the great artists who've painted masterpieces here in the Latin Quarter!" Mrs. Bobbsey remarked as they came out of the restaurant.

"I wonder if there are any great ones painting here right now?" Nan mused dreamily. "I mean *future* great artists who aren't famous yet."

"Too bad we can't spot one," joked Mr. Bobbsey. "We might be able to pick up a real bargain!"

Flossie pointed to a tall, openwork metal tower thrusting skyward in the distance. It seemed to dominate the whole city of Paris. "What's that, Daddy?"

"The Eiffel Tower. It was built by the

same man who rigged the steel framework that holds up our Statue of Liberty. In fact it was France that gave America the lady with the torch."

With no tour schedule to hinder them, the Bobbseys strolled about on a pleasantly zigzag course. They knew that in whatever direction they walked, there were sure to be interesting sights ahead.

Here and there among the famous old streets lined with typical Parisian shops, stood dazzling modern buildings. When the younger twins tired of walking or of riding on their father's shoulders, Mr. Bobbsey hailed a taxi and invited the driver to give them his own guided tour of Paris.

The traffic was horrendous. Sometimes their cab had to slow to a crawl, while at others, cars darted in and out of different lanes at reckless speed amid furious honking.

By the time the Bobbseys returned to their hotel, they felt as if they had crammed a whole week's worth of sightseeing into one afternoon. Among the landmarks they had viewed were the Arch of Triumph, the Louvre museum, the Paris Opera, the Luxembourg Palace and Gardens, and the popular new transparent Pompidou art center, with its visible metal skeleton and an escalator crawling up the front like a glass caterpillar.

In the hotel lobby, Nan hurried to the reception desk to get their room keys. "Were there any calls or messages for us while we were out?" she inquired hopefully.

The clerk checked the pigeonhole boxes behind the counter and shook his head. "No, mam'zelle—nothing at all."

Nan turned away, disappointed and a bit worried. *What on earth could have happened to Julie Palmer?*

Bert seemed to sense the anxious thoughts that were going through his sister's mind. "Who do you suppose that red-haired woman was who spoke to you at the airport?" he mused aloud as they joined

33

the rest of the family in front of the elevator.

"I wish I knew," Nan murmured. "Whoever she was, she seemed to know all about that crook who tried to steal the perfume Julie sent me."

"And there's another good question," said Bert. "*Why* did he try to steal it?"

Back in Lakeport, the Bobbseys were famous for their knack of unraveling mysteries. In fact they seemed to *attract* mysteries wherever they went. And now, on their first day in France, a new one was already taking shape!

Mrs. Bobbsey had spent a year at the University of Grenoble in France during her college days. While there, she had made friends with another student, Colette Duclos, who was now a successful businesswoman in Paris and ran her own advertising agency.

Not knowing Colette's office address or the name of her company, Mary Bobbsey had been unable to telephone her sooner. But now she decided to find out if her old friend might have arrived home.

Kicking off her shoes, she picked up the telephone and asked the operator to put through a call. To her delight, Colette Duclos answered on the first ring.

"Mary, *ma chérie!*" the Frenchwoman exclaimed. "What are you doing in Paris?"

"Enjoying our summer vacation."

"But why did you not let me know you were coming?"

"Oh dear, I should have, but I was so busy getting myself and the children ready! I know you must be terribly busy, too, Colette, but could you possibly spare time to see us tomorrow?"

"Tomorrow? What is wrong with to-night?"

"No, no—this is much too short notice," Mrs. Bobbsey protested. "Dick and I are just going to slip out with the children and—"

"Do not talk nonsense," Colette Duclos

35

said firmly. "You will all be my guests tonight at dinner—I insist on it! How soon shall I expect you?"

In the end, Mrs. Bobbsey happily gave in. It was agreed that they would meet at Madame Duclos's apartment at 8:00.

Mr. and Mrs. Bobbsey and the two girls occupied bedrooms of the same suite, with a sitting room in between, while Bert and Freddie shared a room of their own across the hall.

So far, none of the family seemed to be suffering from jet lag. After catching forty winks while awaiting their turn in the bath or shower, everyone was looking forward to the evening ahead by the time they were dressed and ready to start.

"It's only 7:15, Mom," said Nan. "Do you think we might have time to stop at Julie's place first and find out what's wrong?"

"Did you try calling her, dear?"

"Yes, I did, but the operator said there's no such name in the Paris directory."

"Hmm, well then, I suppose we might look in, if it's not too far out of our way."

Julie Palmer's address turned out to be a rooming house in a working-class section of Paris called the 11th Arrondissement. The concierge, or landlady, was a gaunt, gray-haired woman with several gold teeth. Despite her rather dragonish look, her manner was kindly and helpful.

"Do I not know you, my dear?" she puzzled on discovering that Nan was American. "Ah, but of course! If you are a friend of Mam'zelle Julie's, then you must be the girl in that photo she showed me not long ago! *Quel dommage!* What a pity she did not know you were coming to visit her!"

"But she *did* know!" Nan said unhappily.

The concierge looked astonished. "But how can that be? Mam'zelle Julie left on a trip just the day before yesterday—and she said nothing about expecting any American visitors!"

.4.

Excitement
on the Seine

"That's crazy!" Flossie blurted. "Why
would Miss Palmer go on a trip after she
phoned all the way across the ocean to say
she'd meet us at the airport?"

"It is indeed strange," said the concierge. Then she shrugged her shoulders and spread her hands in a typically
French way. "Still, who is to know these
days what any young woman will do, or
why?"

"Did she say *where* she was going, or

how long she expected to be gone?" Nan asked.

"Alas, no, mam'zelle—in fact she spoke as if she wished to keep her trip a secret. She said only that she might be gone for several weeks."

"Several *weeks!*" Nan echoed in dismay —at that rate, she might never see her friend during the Bobbseys' vacation in France!

"Do not be upset, *ma petite,*" said the concierge, taking Nan's hand and giving it a motherly pat. "If you will tell me where you are staying, and Mam'zelle Palmer returns sooner, I will tell her to call you at once!"

"That's very kind of you," added Mrs. Bobbsey, who had come in with Nan and Flossie while Mr. Bobbsey and the two boys waited outside in the taxi. She told the concierge the name of their hotel, then said, "Come along, girls. We'd better be going on to Colette Duclos's apartment."

Nan looked downcast as they drove away.

"How come Miss Palmer wasn't there?" Freddie asked.

"Her landlady said she went away on a trip," Flossie replied—and added with a wise six-year-old look, "But I think something *funny's* going on!"

"Like what?" said Bert.

"How do I know? But Miss Palmer promised Freddie on the phone that she'd meet us, and she didn't show up, and now it turns out she's not even home. That doesn't make sense. Miss Palmer wouldn't tell fibs!"

Bert looked at his twin. "You think something's happened to her, Nan?"

Nan's forehead puckered in a worried frown. "I can't think of any other reason why she wouldn't keep her word."

"Do you suppose she's been kidnapped?"

"Now wait a minute, son," Mr. Bobbsey interrupted. "Let's not let our imaginations

40

run away with us just because of a slight mixup."

"That's what I can't understand," Nan puzzled. "Her landlady spoke as if Julie just went away by herself—of her own accord. She didn't say anybody *took* her away, or *made* her go."

"Of course not," Mrs. Bobbsey said soothingly. "There's probably some simple explanation. I'm sure we'll hear from Miss Palmer very soon . . . maybe tomorrow."

"I remember now," Freddie hissed to Flossie, loud enough for everyone else to hear, "when I talked to her on the phone, she sounded *worried!*"

"Now, Freddie—!" his mother warned, and shook a finger at him.

Mary Bobbsey's college friend lived in a fashionable neighborhood on the west side of Paris. Her apartment building was on the Avenue Foch, within sight of the tall trees in the lovely wooded park called the Bois de Boulogne.

Colette Duclos herself was a tall, attractive blond woman. Mrs. Bobbsey had explained to the twins that, although she was not married, she was usually called Madame rather than Mademoiselle Duclos for business reasons, being the head of her own company.

"My dear Mary, what a wonderful family you and Richard have!" she exclaimed, gazing at the twins with an envious smile.

She kissed Nan and shook hands with Bert and made a special fuss over Flossie and Freddie because of their curly blond hair. "I wish you were my very own!" she said, hugging the little twins.

Freddie, as usual when hugged, made a face, but secretly enjoyed being fussed over. "She wears perfume, too!" he whispered to Flossie.

"Mm, I know—she smells nice!"

Colette Duclos smiled and hugged them again. "First let us make ourselves comfortable while I hear all about you Bobbseys and Lakeport," she said. "And then I shall tell you about my life here in Paris, and presently we shall go and dine."

They ate in a restaurant called *Le Vieux Galion*, which was actually a huge galleon moored on a lake in the Bois, near the Longchamps racecourse. Madame Duclos plied the Bobbseys with questions and told them about her work at the advertising agency.

"It seems so long since we were at the university together, Mary *ma chérie*," she sighed to Mrs. Bobbsey. "I cannot tell you how happy I am to see you again. And I am so eager to show you all around Paris!"

Mrs. Bobbsey smiled back apologetically. "It's lovely of you to suggest such a thing, Colette, but I'm afraid we add up to too big a crowd for that—especially with four lively children to keep tabs on."

"*Mais non*—that is no problem, Mary!" the Frenchwoman insisted. "Already I have the perfect answer!"

She explained that her niece Odile, who

worked as a copywriter at her ad agency, was engaged to a young sailor named André, who was now on leave from the French Navy.

"Odile is dying for an excuse to get away from the office, so she can spend more time with him. I will assign her and André to act as tour guide for the twins. Believe me, she will be delighted—and meanwhile I shall be your and Richard's personal tour guide!"

The twins' parents flashed each other a questioning look, then grinned. "How can we refuse," Mr. Bobbsey said with a twinkle, "when she twists our arms so charmingly?"

Before taking them back to the hotel in her car, Colette gave the Bobbseys a spectacular tour of Paris by night.

From the Arc de Triomphe on the Place Charles de Gaulle—which used to be called the Place de l'Etoile, or Star Plaza, because of the twelve avenues radiating out from it like rays of starlight—she drove them along the glittering Champs-Elysees to the Place de la Concorde, marked by an obelisk, or stone needle, carved with hieroglyphs. She told the twins Napoleon had brought it back from a war in Egypt.

To wind up the tour, she also drove them past some of the famous Parisian nightspots like the Moulin Rouge and the Crazy Horse, as well as that center of Paris night life, the Place Pigalle.

Next morning, the Bobbseys enjoyed breakfast in their rooms. It consisted of hot chocolate and croissants. Flossie licked her lips. "Ummm, that's about the yummiest breakfast I ever ate!"

But when they compared notes later, Bert just shrugged. "It was okay—but personally I prefer Dinah's pancakes and bacon."

"Ditto," his dad agreed.

The twins' two tour guides soon arrived. Odile proved to be a pretty blond girl who looked like her Aunt Colette. The Bobbseys learned that she attended classes part time at the Sorbonne, a famous college of the University of Paris. Her boyfriend, André, a dark-haired young man from Marseilles in the south of France, was wearing his Navy uniform, with its white sailor hat topped by a red pompom.

"We thought today you might like to go for a boat ride on the Seine," Odile suggested.

Nan clapped her hands. "Oh, yes! That sounds like fun!"

At a landing near the Solferino Bridge in the center of Paris, they got on a wide, glass-enclosed sightseeing barge called a bateau-mouche. André led them topside to seats like the ones upstairs on a double-decker bus. "Hooray! We can see everything from here!" crowed Freddie.

There was plenty to see on both sides of the river, but just gliding along was a pleasure in itself. The street embankments were green with ivy, and fishermen waved to them from the quays along the water.

The boat circled the Ile de la Cité, the island on which stands the majestic Cathedral of Notre Dame. "We'll take you there tomorrow," Odile promised.

After looping around the island, they started back downstream. Just as they were approaching a bridge, Freddie gave a cry of excitement. "Look!" he pointed. "It's *her!*"

On the bridge, a baldheaded man was squabbling with a woman with red hair!

.5.

A Strange Drawing

"Hey, Freddie's right!" Bert exclaimed. "That's the woman who spoke to you at the airport, Nan—the redhead who knew all about the thief who tried to swipe your perfume!"

"Yes, she *is* the same one!" Nan gasped.

Odile and Andre were confused, and the Bobbseys hastily explained.

Meanwhile, the quarrel on the bridge was rapidly turning into an outright scuffle. The bald man, who looked mean and tough, now seemed to be trying to snatch the red-haired woman's handbag. She was holding it as far out of his reach as she could, and pushing him away with her other hand.

"Oh no, she dropped it!" wailed Flossie.

By this time, the bateau-mouche was passing under the bridge. The Bobbseys and their two friends saw the bag plunge downward and land on the very edge of the quay!

Freddie immediately clamored for the boat to stop. Odile and André looked embarrassed, while Bert and Nan tried to shush their little brother.

"Calm down, Freddie!" Bert growled under his breath. "So she lost her purse— there's nothing we can do about it!"

"Yes, there is!" Freddie insisted. "If they'll just stop the boat, I can run back and get it!"

The other passengers were looking amused and sympathetic. One of the boat's crew came to see what all the commotion was about. In the end, with a typically Parisian shrug and tilt of the eyebrow, he

arranged for the bateau-mouche to pull over to the quay so the Bobbseys and their friends could disembark.

Freddie dashed back under the bridge, as fast as he could, to the other side. "Oh, gosh!" he muttered. "Maybe I'm too late!"

The bag had landed not only on the edge of the quay, but wide open, and some of its contents had spilled out.

His eyes widened as he saw an object slowly sliding out of the bag. It looked as if it might be heavy—maybe a gun!—Freddie couldn't be sure. Whatever it was, it had snagged on the handbag's lining.

Freddie pumped his short legs even harder and faster, but it was no use. The lining suddenly ripped and the object plopped down into the water, pulling the bag over the edge with it!

Freddie reached the scene just in time to witness the splash. "Oh, *no-o-o!*" he groaned out loud.

Without even stopping to think, the boy

51

flopped down on the wet, mossy stone quay to try and fish up the handbag. It seemed to have lost enough of its heavier contents to float—at least for a while.

Freddie leaned far out and reached down as far as he could. The river was high enough so that he could almost touch the water with his fingertips.

"Freddie—don't!" Nan screamed, and Bert chimed in even louder. "Stop it, you little nut! Get away from the edge!"

"Don't worry—I won't fall over!" he called back. The bag was almost within reach, if he could just stretch out an inch or two farther . . . !

André didn't waste any breath shouting. Having longer legs than the others, he concentrated on reaching the scene as fast as possible.

He arrived a split second too late. Just as he was about to grab Freddie's ankle the little boy lost his balance. *Ker-plunk!* he toppled into the water with a mighty splash!

52

"Freddie-e-e!" his little twin screeched. Clutching her chubby cheeks in dismay, Flossie hopped up and down with fear for her brother's safety. "Save him, Mister André!" she yelled. "Please save him!"

"Have no fear, *ma petite*," the sailor replied calmly. "I will jump in myself if necessary—but first let us try this way."

Pulling off his blouse, he flung it out from the quay, holding onto one sleeve.

Freddie was splashing about wildly and still trying to reach the handbag. A piece of paper was sticking out of it.

"Never mind her bag!" Bert shouted in exasperation. "Just grab hold of André's shirtsleeve!"

Somehow Freddie managed to do both. He was clutching the handbag triumphantly as Andre hauled him in closer to the quay and hoisted him out of the water.

"Oh, Freddie, you dear little idiot!" Nan exclaimed, hugging him in relief in spite of his wetness. "What makes you get into so much trouble?!"

"I'm okay. I can swim, you know!" the young boy retorted indignantly. "And I saved the lady's purse, didn't I?"

"Yes, and a fat lot of good it did," said Bert. "Looks like she's gone."

To make sure, he hurried up the stone steps leading to the top of the bridge. As expected, neither the red-haired woman nor her bald enemy was anywhere in sight.

After shaking his head and waving his arms criss-cross to signal *No luck*, Bert went back down to the quay.

By now, André and Odile had dried Freddie off a bit and wrung as much water as they could out of his clothing. Then Nan suggested looking in the handbag for anything that might help to identify its owner.

It still contained a few items, including a comb, a ballpoint pen, and a small change purse, but nothing such as a driver's license or credit card that might have shown the red-haired woman's name or address.

Nan, however, was staring with a puzzled frown at the piece of paper that Freddie had seen sticking out of the bag. "Look at this," she said.

Although partly wet, the paper bore a drawing that could still be clearly read. It showed a weird-looking, big-nosed face with wild eyebrows, pointed ears and a tongue sticking out of its grinning mouth.

"Look at that!" Flossie murmured. "That guy really looks crazy!"

"You said it," Freddie agreed. "And what do those numbers mean?"

Underneath the drawing of the face were the numerals 1145. Neither Nan nor Bert could supply an answer.

"You can puzzle over that later," said Odile gently. "For now I think we should get Freddie back to your hotel and into some dry clothes."

Afterwards, they lunched at a students' cafe where Odile often ate. Then they boarded another bateau-mouche, and this time completed their sightseeing cruise without incident.

It was only mid-afternoon, so Nan asked

1145

if they could go to Julie Palmer's rooming house and see if the concierge had any news of her missing tenant.

"Okay," said André. "How would you like a ride on the Metro?"

"What's that?" asked Bert.

"Our subway."

The underground train was clean and fast. In no time at all, it seemed, they emerged near the rooming house on a street called the Rue de Malte.

"Alas, no, *chérie*," the concierge told Nan. "I have heard nothing at all from Mam'zelle Julie."

"Oh, gosh . . . !" Nan's lips quivered and she blinked back tears. The more she thought about what had happened at the airport, and the struggle on the bridge, the more certain she felt that something was wrong—very wrong.

What if her teacher friend had had an accident, or had indeed fallen into the hands of kidnappers?!

"C-C-Couldn't we please look in her

apartment?" Nan begged. "I mean—just to make sure she's not there, or didn't leave a note for us, or something?"

The concierge hesitated. Privately, she too was a bit worried about the missing young American. *"Eh bien,"* she said at last. "Perhaps it will do no harm to look."

She led them up to the third floor and knocked on Julie Palmer's door. There was no answer, so she took out a large key ring and opened the door.

Everyone gasped as they looked inside. *The place had been ransacked!*

.6.

Dream Flower

"I *knew* something was wrong!" Nan cried.

The Bobbseys, Odile and André hastily followed the concierge into Julie's apartment. It was very small, consisting of a bed-sitting room and a kitchenette. The foldup bed had been pulled down and the bedding torn apart, drawers had been yanked out and emptied, and everything was strewn in wild disorder.

"Name of a name, what has happened?!" the elderly Frenchwoman exclaimed, holding her head with both hands.

"There's how the robber got in and out," Bert said, pointing to an open window. When he looked outside, he saw that there was a narrow alleyway below and, at one side of the window, a rickety fire escape.

The concierge was gazing around with a look of horror and muttering to herself in French as she surveyed the mess. "I had better call the police *tout de suite!*" she announced, and bustled out of the apartment. Moments later, the Bobbseys could hear her talking rapidly on a pay phone that they had noticed at the front of the hall.

"What could the thief have been after to make him tear the place apart this way?" Odile wondered aloud.

Nan and Bert exchanged glances, each thinking the same thing. Before either could speak, Flossie blurted, "Maybe that perfume Miss Palmer sent you, Nan!"

The older Bobbsey girl nodded and pinched her upper lip thoughtfully. "Could be. Maybe Julie kept some here in her apartment."

60

Two policemen soon arrived, one in uniform and one a plain-clothes detective. They looked over the scene of the crime, and the detective asked questions and took notes.

Neither spoke English, so Odile had to tell the twins what was being said.

"We will certainly try to catch whoever pulled this break-in," the detective remarked, closing up his notebook. "But it won't be easy—especially if you do not even know for sure whether anything was taken."

Nan touched Odile's arm. "What about Julie Palmer? Aren't they going to try and find her?"

Odile spoke in French to the detective, who replied with a shrug.

"Miss Palmer told the concierge she was going away, so she cannot be classified as a missing person, and we have no reason yet to take any action," Odile translated.

The twins were unhappy over the way things had turned out. Nan feared more than ever that her teacher-friend might be in trouble or danger—or worse yet, that something bad might already have happened to her.

"Where did Miss Palmer work?" she asked the concierge after the police had gone, and the visitors had restored some order to Julie's rooms.

"Right, we need to check that out," said Bert. "Miss Palmer was a chemist, so she may have had a job in a laboratory somewhere in Paris. Even if she was making the perfume all by herself, she'd need some place to do it other than right here in her apartment, wouldn't she?"

"*Oui*, that is so," the elderly Frenchwoman replied. "Mam'zelle Palmer rented a laboratory in the twentieth arrondissement. I never thought of it before, but you might look for her there. If you come downstairs to my rooms, I will find the address for you."

As they left the rooming house twenty

minutes later, Flossie nudged her big sister.

"Nan, is this Miss Palmer's handwriting?" She held out a scrap of paper that bore two names, *Mimi Redon* and *Philippe St. Yves*. Each was followed by numbers that Nan thought might be telephone numbers.

"Yes, it *is* her writing! Where'd you get this, Floss?" she asked in surprise.

"It was lying on the floor in all that mess back at Miss Palmer's place."

Nan gave her golden-haired little sister a quick hug. "You're a smart girl, honey! This may be an important clue!"

The twentieth arrondissement of Paris lay just east of the eleventh, where Julie's rooming house was located. Her lab turned out to be a single room on the ground floor of a grimy industrial building.

André scouted around for the caretaker. He proved to be a limping, elderly man who answered to the name of Papa Louie.

He wore a tattered beret, and his good-natured face was stubbled with gray whiskers.

"*Bonjour, bonjour, mes amis!*" he greeted his visitors, reaching out with a smile to tousle Freddie's blond mop. "And what can Papa Louie do for all you fine folk today, eh?"

Odile explained why they had come.

"Mam'zelle Julie? *Mais non,*" the caretaker puckered his brow and rubbed his bristly jaw, "I have not seen her for, let me think, at least three days."

Since he could speak English, Nan told him how worried she was for Miss Palmer's safety. An expression of concern came over the elderly man's face and he readily agreed to let the Bobbseys see her lab.

It looked much as the twins had expected, with a well-lighted workbench laden with racks of test tubes, Bunsen burners, retorts and distilling apparatus.

There was no need to check the bottles

and jars on the shelves. The fragrance that greeted their nostrils on entering the laboratory seemed to confirm what the Bobbseys had already guessed.

"Was Miss Palmer making perfume?" Nan asked.

"Ah, *oui!* Is it not a lovely scent?" Papa Louie's face lit up and he waved his arm around as if to stir up the fragrance wafting on the still air of the laboratory. He began chattily telling his visitors about the long hours Julie worked and the experiments she conducted day after day, trying to concoct a new perfume more alluring than any now in the stores, while they all looked around the laboratory.

In his fatherly way, it seemed, Papa Louie had become very attached to the young American chemist, and she in turn trusted and confided in him. He spoke as proudly of her work as if she were his own daughter.

"Would you believe?" he boasted, "two

65

famous companies here in Paris wish to buy the formula of the new perfume Mam'zelle Julie created!"

"Do you know their names?" Bert asked eagerly.

Papa Louie took off his beret and scratched his head. "No, but I can tell you the name she gave her perfume. She christened it *Fleur de Reve!*"

"Dream Flower," Odile translated.

"What a beautiful name!" said Nan. "If two companies want to buy the formula for Dream Flower, it must be very valuable. Where does she keep the perfume?"

"*Mais oui,* it is *trés* valuable! So valuable, in fact, she always keeps the flask of *Fleur de Reve* that she made up in that safe over th—"

As he turned and pointed, the old man suddenly gasped in dismay. The door of the rusty old safe standing in one corner of the lab was hanging slightly ajar.

Both Bert and Nan rushed to look inside. *The safe was empty!*

. 7 .

Perfume People

"The safe has been robbed!" Papa Louie exclaimed, hobbling closer to peer over the twins' shoulders.

"And the Dream Flower perfume's gone!" Nan said sadly. There was no longer any doubt in her mind that Julie Palmer was the victim of some criminal plot.

"Don't worry, Sis," Bert muttered, squeezing her hand when he saw how worried she looked. "We'll solve this mystery yet and find Miss Palmer!"

Freddie piped up, "Hey, look at this!"

He was holding a coin that was stamped with what the older twins guessed was Arabic script. It also bore the numeral 50.

"It is Algerian," said André. "A fifty-centime piece—half a dinar. I have seen them in North Africa."

"Where'd you find it?" Bert asked.

"On the floor. Is it valuable?"

"Not very, I am afràid, *mon ami*," André told the little boy.

"Never mind—stick it in your pocket," said Bert. "It may be a clue."

Over dinner that evening, the twins related their adventures to Mr. and Mrs. Bobbsey and Colette Duclos. The family was entertaining their French friend on the terrace of a famed Parisian restaurant, *La Closerie des Lilas.*

"This begins to sound like a case for the Surèté," said Madame Duclos.

"What's that?" asked Freddie.

"France's most famous detective force. I believe it is somewhat like your American F.B.I." With a smile, she added, "But

69

then, from all I hear, you Bobbsey twins are first-rate detectives yourselves!"

Nan and Bert flushed and tried not to look too pleased, but Flossie grinned brightly and asked, "How'd you find out?"

"By reading the newspaper clippings your mother sends me now and then about the mysteries you have solved in Lake-port."

Mr. Bobbsey chuckled. "Nothing like having your own publicity agent, eh, kids?"

"Well, it's true just the same," Mrs. Bobbsey said proudly. "They've solved some cases that have even baffled the po-lice."

"You bet they have," her husband beamed. "In fact they're one of the Bobbsey Lumberyard's best advertise-ments. Some of my customers talk more about the twins than they do about the lumber I'm trying to sell them!"

By now, Nan was so embarrassed that

she tried to change the subject. "Do you know anything about the perfume business, Aunt Colette?"

"A little, yes. Sometimes I create magazine ads for cosmetic companies. Why do you ask?"

"Well, that old man, Papa Louie, who let us into Julie Palmer's lab, told us two famous companies in Paris are interested in buying the formula for her new perfume . . ."

Nan took something out of her purse, then went on, "And Flossie found this paper in Julie's apartment with two names on it. I was wondering if they might be connected with those companies Papa Louie mentioned."

Madame Duclos's eyes widened. "You are indeed quite a sleuth, *chérie!* These are two of the most important people your friend could hope to deal with!"

Mimi Redon, she explained, was head of a cosmetics firm called *Mimi et Compagnie.*

"A very tough cookie, that one. And Philippe St. Yves is a world-famous fashion designer."

"My goodness, yes," said Mrs. Bobbsey. "Some of his designs get shown even in Lakeport, though I'm not sure we'll ever be rich enough for me to afford one of his little numbers!"

"He is into many things besides clothing," Colette Duclos went on. "I have heard talk that his fashion house may soon bring out a perfume that will bear the St. Yves name."

She gave Nan a keen look and added, "Mind you, I am not personally acquainted with either Madame Mimi or M'sieu St. Yves, but I do know some of their advertising people. If I can help in any way, I will be happy to do so."

"Hmm, that's an idea!" said Nan. "Let me think about it, Aunt Colette. Thanks a lot!"

Later on, while the adults were chatting and paying attention to the younger twins,

Nan held a brief whispered conversation with Bert. Then, before leaving the restaurant, she found a chance to speak privately to the Frenchwoman. "Could you sort of drop a hint to someone you know at each of those two companies, Aunt Colette?"

"Of course, my dear. What would you like me to say?"

"That two Americans want to tell Madame Mimi and Mr. St. Yves something important about Julie Palmer's new perfume."

"In just those words?"

Nan blushed a bit nervously and said, "Yes, if you don't mind. And say we are now in Paris and may drop in soon."

Madame Duclos's eyes sparkled. "I shall phone them first thing in the morning, *chérie!* Something tells me that two young American detectives are hot on the trail of their missing friend!"

"By the way, can you tell us their addresses?"

"Yes, they are both near the Place Vendome. I will write down the addresses."

Next day at breakfast, Nan and Bert busily studied the guidebooks their parents had brought, and a map of Paris. When Odile and André arrived, the couple suggested going first to the Tuileries Gardens, a beautifully landscaped panorama of flowers, fountains and lawns. There, the younger twins could watch an open-air Punch-and-Judy show and have fun at the children's playground.

Freddie and Flossie enthusiastically agreed, but the older twins asked if they could make two brief stops on the way.

"*Oui,* if you like," replied Odile, with a smile. "André and I are in no hurry."

The older twins quickly found a taxi and Nan gave the driver the first address Colette had written down. It was a dazzling shop on the Rue de la Paix, whose awning bore the name MIMI ET CIE in smart gold letters.

"Look, there's no need for you guys to

come in with us," Nan told the younger twins, who had tumbled out of the taxi with their siblings. "Why don't you all go on to the Tuileries and we'll meet you at the playground in, say, half an hour?"

After promising to be careful and to take a taxi directly to the gardens when they were finished, Nan and Bert waved to their companions and turned to the business at hand.

A giant doorman in a white, gold-braided uniform saluted the two youngsters and greeted them with a smiling remark in French. When they replied in English, he switched to that language. "May I help you, Mam'zelle et M'sieu?"

"We'd like to see Madame Mimi, if you please," said Nan.

"Ah, I see. She is a very busy person, you know. Is she expecting you?"

"*Oui*, I believe she may be," Nan said, trying to smile confidently. "Please tell her the two Americans Colette Duclos spoke of have arrived—and please say it just like that."

"*Très bien.*" He lifted a white phone nestled in one corner of the shop entrance and spoke into it for a while. Then he hung up and opened the door for Nan and Bert with another smiling salute. "Madame's office is on the fifth floor!"

Inside, the glass counters were glittering with displays of makeup, perfume and hair preparations. The two young visitors were whisked upward by elevator, and presently found themselves being ushered into Madame Mimi's private office.

She was a hawk-faced woman in a silver lamé jumpsuit with rhinestoned glasses and lacquered, jet-black hair. She sprang up from her crystal plastic desk and glared angrily at the twins.

"What is this, some kind of joke? I was told earlier this morning that two Americans had something important to tell me about Julie Palmer's new perfume."

"Yes, ma'am, we do," said Bert.

"Miss Palmer sent me some of that fragrance she created," Nan went on. "But now she's disappeared, and someone has stolen all the rest of the perfume from her lab!"

Madame Mimi seemed to freeze for a moment. Her eyes bored into her two young visitors like gimlets. Finally she hissed:

"I do not know what you are up to, and I have no time to find out, nor do I care. For your information, Mam'zelle Palmer tried to sell me her new fragrance, but I was not interested—for the simple reason that *Mimi et Compagnie* will soon bring out a similar perfume of our own. Now kindly remove yourselves from my office!"

Madame Mimi jabbed a button on her desk. A uniformed flunky quickly escorted the twins downstairs and out of the building.

"That was a short visit," said the doorman.

Bert grinned back. "Sure, we Bobbseys don't waste any time."

But as they walked away, he muttered to Nan, "Whew! That Madame Mimi was a real battleaxe!"

"Never mind," Nan giggled. "At least we found out why Julie had her name written down."

Philippe St. Yves' place of business was nearby. It was a graceful old townhouse. As they were talking to the receptionist, Monsieur St. Yves happened to walk into the front room.

He was a tall, slender man, elegantly dressed in a gray suit and open-necked silk shirt with a red carnation in his buttonhole. He seemed amused by the twins' visit and readily agreed to talk to them.

"Yes, of course, I know Mam'zelle Palmer," he said. "She is a talented *parfumeuse* and her *Fleur de Reve* is a very alluring fragrance. We considered making her an offer for it, but then decided not to."

"Why not?" asked Nan.

"I am sorry, *chérie,* but it was for reasons which I cannot yet talk about."

As they taxied back to the Tuileries Garden, Bert said, "What do you make of that guy, St. Yves, Nan?"

"I'm not sure. He was certainly friendly and he answered our questions nicely enough—all except the last one! I'm still wondering why."

From the Tuileries, Odile and André took the four Bobbsey twins to Notre Dame —the Church of Our Lady of Paris. Visitors flock to this great gray Gothic cathedral from all over the world, and on the day of the Bobbseys' visit, it was swarming with as many people as usual.

They made their way inside through the teeming crowd. The arched ceiling, more than a hundred feet high, seemed so far overhead it was hard to imagine how the oldtime masons, centuries ago, could have lifted the stones into place. Nan gazed in awe at the gorgeous stained-glass rose windows at either side of the cross-shaped church.

Bert was eager to go up into one of the twin towers, where he had seen the Hunchback of Notre Dame madly ringing bells in the movie. From here, they could admire the tall central spire, with the twelve copper Apostles at its base.

One of them, turning as if to peer up at the pinnacle, represents St. Thomas. "But actually," said André, "he was made to look like the architect who rebuilt the tower, Eugene Viollet-le-Duc."

After they had gazed out over Paris from one of the little stone balconies, Odile told the twins it was 11:45 and would soon be time for lunch. As she and André went back inside of the cathedral, Flossie uttered an excited cry:

"Hey, there's that *face!*"

Cathedral Clue

"What face?" Bert asked his little sister.

Flossie was pointing to one of the queer stone monsters, called gargoyles, whose ugly, grinning faces stick out around the cathedral towers. Some serve as drain spouts, others are mere decorations.

Nan was amazed when she saw the one Flossie was pointing at.

"It's just like the funny face on that drawing!" the blond girl declared.

"You know, I think Flossie's right," Nan said.

"'Course I'm right! Take it out and see!"

Nan had carefully salvaged the paper from the wet handbag, hoping it might prove to be a useful clue. And perhaps now her little sister had identified the clue!

Fishing in her own purse, Nan took out the paper and unfolded it. Then she compared the face in the drawing with that of the stone gargoyle.

"Right on, Floss! It's definitely the same face! . . . But why on earth," Nan mused aloud, "would that red-haired woman be carrying a picture of a *gargoyle* around with her?"

"Search me," said Freddie, "but there's a redheaded lady down there right now. Maybe it's her!"

He pointed down at the throng of tourists milling about far below. One of them had dark but vivid red hair that made her especially noticeable. Freddie sounded half joking, and at first the others didn't take him seriously as they gazed down from the tower balcony to see for themselves.

But suddenly there was a flicker of sunlight on lenses as she raised a pair of opera glasses, or binoculars, to peer upward.

"Hey, is she *spying* on us?" exclaimed Freddie. His tone was no longer joking.

"No, her spyglasses aren't pointing at us," said Flossie. "She's looking over *that* way!"

"*Toward the gargoyle!*" Nan gasped.

Bert suddenly clued in. "I've got it!" he blurted, snapping his fingers.

"Got what?" asked Freddie.

"Those numbers underneath the drawing —one, one, four, five."

"What about them?"

"They must stand for the *time*, don't you see? Odile just told us it's eleven-forty-five!"

"Ohmigosh!" said Nan. "You're absolutely right, Bert! Like maybe the time she's supposed to meet someone—"

"Under that particular gargoyle!" said Bert, finishing her thought. "The drawing was a way to show her the meeting place!"

And as Nan nodded excitedly, Flossie got excited, too. "You're right, Bert! You guessed it!" she cried. "She *is* meeting somebody!"

By this time, the redhead had strolled over to a point directly below the gargoyle in question—and now a dark-haired man could be seen walking straight toward her!

A few moments later, they were talking together.

"Now's our chance to find out what her game is!" said Bert. "If that redhead knew all about the airport thief, maybe she knows something about Julie Palmer, too! We've got to get down there fast—before those two get away!"

Odile and André, who had rejoined the twins, now gaped in surprise at the fast-moving young Americans. But they, too, were curious about the meaning of the strange events that seemed to be unfolding before their eyes. So they breathlessly followed the Bobbseys down the steep stone stairs of the cathedral and out onto

85

the pavement of the Place du Parvis outside.

The sunlight was dazzling after the darkness of the church's interior. But it quickly became apparent that they were too late. The plotters—if they *were* plotters—had just separated and were now walking away from each other, the woman in one direction and the dark-haired man in another.

"You follow the redhead, I'll go after the guy!" Bert exclaimed to his sister.

"Right, chief!"

Before either Odile or André could object, the two older twins were off and running.

The man was heading off into the maze of narrow streets north of the cathedral—all that remains now of what was once the Ile de la Cité's medieval quarter.

Bert groaned in frustration as he glimpsed a parked motorcycle ahead. There was no chance of catching his quarry now. The man leaped astride the bike's saddle, gunned the engine and took off with a thunderous roar of exhaust!

But for one brief moment before he disappeared from view, Bert saw something that made his heart beat faster. The chase had definitely not been a waste of time!

Bert returned to the main entrance of the cathedral where André and Odile were waiting with the little twins. Nan came back almost at the same time, looking disappointed and out of breath.

"No luck?" her twin inquired.

She shook her head glumly. "I lost her in a crowd of tourists. How about you?"

Bert grinned. "I got a look at the guy's face—and guess what?"

"I give up."

"He has a bushy black mustache!"

It took a second or two for Nan to catch on. Then her face brightened with excitement. "The sneak thief at the airport!"

"Right! So the redhead *must* know something about Julie Palmer!"

After lunch, the twins rejoined their parents at the hotel for an afternoon of family shopping and sightseeing. But it was arranged that next day the young French couple would escort them to the Louvre and take them up in the Eiffel Tower.

"Wow!" Freddie exclaimed the following morning as they approached the Louvre. "This place looks *huge!* Are we going to walk all through it?"

André chuckled. "Do not worry—this is the world's biggest art museum. We could not possibly see it all in one day!"

At first a fortress, then a palace, the Louvre is actually a double chain of buildings that were added on to, century after century. On one side, they stretch along the Seine for nearly half a mile—every room filled with art treasures.

Nan was eager to see the famous portrait by Leonardo da Vinci called the Mona Lisa. But so many people were lined up to see it that, instead, the Bobbseys and their two friends just gave up and strolled about, viewing the paintings, sculpture and other works of art.

Bert looked around as he felt a tap on the shoulder. A student painter, with a canvas and folding easel under one arm, was holding out a note. *"Excusez-moi, mon ami.* Are you one of the Bobbsey family?"

"Yes . . . why?"

"Then this is for you."

Bert took the note uncertainly. "Who sent it? I mean—where'd you get it?"

"A man pointed you out and paid me to deliver it just a few moments ago."

"What man? Where is he?"

The artist shrugged. "I do not know. He just spoke to me and paid me and then walked away quickly. I do not see him now. All I can tell you is that he was bald."

Bald! Bert shot a startled glance at his twin. Both were wondering the same thing. *Could the sender have been the same bald-headed man they saw struggling with the red-haired woman on the bridge?!*

. 9 .

S.O.S. Eiffel Tower

"Open it, open it!" Freddie urged his big brother excitedly.

The student painter had already walked off across the gallery. Now he was setting up his easel and preparing to copy one of the museum's masterpieces.

Bert unfolded and read the note, then passed it around.

"What does it say?" asked Flossie.

"To go to a certain telephone booth and wait."

"Which booth?"

"Near that door we came in. There's a little map with an arrow to show me the right one."

"Then let's go!" said Freddie impatiently, standing first on one foot, then on the other.

Bert glanced again at Nan, as he always did when uncertain of his next move. In some ways, he trusted his twin's judgment more than he did his own.

"What do you think, Nan?"

"I don't see why not," she shrugged. "We might learn something."

Odile and André had no objection, either, so they trooped to the phone booth and Bert waited inside. Nan squeezed in beside him. Presently the telephone rang.

Bert snatched it up. "Hello?"

"You are Bert Bobbsey?" The voice sounded rough and gravelly and spoke with a French accent.

"That's right," Bert replied. "Who are you?"

"Do not waste time asking foolish questions. Just listen carefully. Your friend, Julie Palmer is in bad trouble—her life is in danger. Are you interested in helping her?"

Nan had her ear pressed to the phone. She nodded emphatically at her twin.

"Yes, we're interested," said Bert. "What about it?"

"I have some valuable information to sell. Information that will help you find her. Perhaps we can make a deal."

"What kind of deal?"

"Do not expect me to talk about it over the phone!" the caller snarled. "You think I am a fool? If you wish to learn my terms, we must meet face to face."

"Where?" Bert asked.

"In Buttes-Chaumont Park. Meet me at the boat landing on the lake in half an hour. And do not call the police, or try to trap me! If I see any suspicious-looking adults hovering around you, the deal is off, and you will never see Julie Palmer alive again! Do you understand?"

A receiver clicked at the other end of the line as the unknown caller hung up.

"I'm going with you, Bert!" Nan exclaimed after he had related the conversation to the others. "And we'd better start right away!"

"Oh no, my dear—you will do no such thing, either of you," Odile said firmly. "This man you are supposed to meet may be a criminal. If he is indeed that bald-headed man we saw on the bridge, he may be extremely dangerous!"

"But we *must* go!" Nan pleaded, almost tearfully. "It may be the only way we can save Julie!"

After a heated discussion, Odile called the restaurant where her aunt usually lunched. It was nearly noon, and there was a chance Madame Duclos might be there with her two American guests.

Odile's hunch paid off, and she was soon able to get Mr. Bobbsey on the phone. At first he, too, was strongly against any meeting with the mysterious caller, but after urgent pleading by both the older twins, he reconsidered.

"Hmm, tell you what. I'll meet you at the park myself. Take a taxi there and wait for me at the park entrance. Repeat—the park *entrance!* Don't go inside till I arrive and can keep an eye on you!"

Bert and Nan obeyed. Buttes-Chaumont Park proved to be an inviting expanse of greenery, with a steep, wooded hill crowned by a little summerhouse, or belvedere, that looked like a miniature Greek temple.

"Looks like Dad hasn't arrived yet," Bert muttered as they stood waiting and gazing around.

Suddenly he felt something hard jab him in the back, and the same voice he had heard on the phone growled, "If you know what's good for you, don't turn around— and that goes for your sister, too!"

As the twins stiffened in fear, the voice went on, "Figured you'd trick me, eh, by waiting here for someone to tail you when you go inside to the boat landing. Well, you're out of luck, *mes enfants*, because that's not where we're going at all! . . . *Start walking!*"

The little twins were having lunch with Odile and André at a restaurant near the Louvre. It had been arranged that they would wait there to hear from Nan and Bert, or from Mr. Bobbsey.

The older twins were to rejoin them at the restaurant after returning from the Parc des Buttes-Chaumont. Otherwise, if delayed past 1:30, they would meet the others on the Eiffel Tower.

"Do you suppose Nan and Bert are all right?" Flossie asked anxiously as she finished the bowl of strawberries that she had chosen for dessert.

"Of course they are, *ma petite*," Odile replied, reaching out to pat the little girl's hand. "Nothing bad can happen while your daddy is watching them."

Moments later, a waiter came to their

table and told André he was wanted on the telephone. When the sailor returned from taking the call, he looked uneasy.

"Nothing is wrong, I hope?" said Odile.

"Er, not really. But there has been a slight mixup. For some reason the twins did not meet M'sieu Bobbsey at the park entrance, as planned. No doubt they are somewhere inside, so a search is now being made for them. He said to tell Freddie and Flossie not to worry, and that we should go on to the Eiffel Tower in case the older twins go there."

At that very moment, Bert and Nan were in a strange room in another part of Paris. They had been taken there by their captor and tied to chairs. Both were struggling to get loose, but trying not to make any noise.

"Are you making any progress?" Nan called out softly to her brother.

"A little. I tried to keep my wrists apart while they were tying me, so the ropes wouldn't be too tight, like you read about in that detective book—and it helped, I think."

"Same here! I've wriggled about half of one hand free!"

Twenty minutes later, both had gotten their hands loose and were able to untie themselves from their chairs.

"So far, so good!" murmured Bert. "Now all we have to do is figure some way to get out of here."

"He locked the door, so it'll have to be out the window," said Nan. "If we're lucky, maybe there's a fire escape!"

The twins spoke in whispers, since their captor had warned them someone would be on guard outside the door at all times.

The third-floor room was evidently at a corner of the building, with a window in each wall. But the blinds were drawn, keeping the room in shadow.

They raised the blinds cautiously, then groaned inwardly in disappointment. Both windows were barred! The two youngsters waved their arms and gesticulated wildly, trying to be noticed by some of the passers-by on the sidewalk below. But nobody paid the slightest attention.

"Oh golly, what'll we do, Bert?" said Nan, her hopes fading. "We daren't knock on the window pane, or that creep outside the door may hear us!"

It was a bright afternoon, but the sunshine outside did nothing to raise their spirits. In the distance, the Eiffel Tower was clearly in view, and suddenly an idea occurred to Bert.

"Still got your purse, Nan?"

"Sure, why?"

"Got a mirror in it?"

Nan nodded and felt a fresh thrill of hope as she clued in. "But how can you aim it?" she asked excitedly.

"Watch me." Bert took out his pocket knife and cut a hole in the blind through which he could glimpse the Eiffel Tower when the blind was pulled down. Sunshine was blazing in strongly through the other window, and he left that blind up.

Then he held Nan's mirror at an angle so as to reflect the sunshine toward the covered window. A bright spot of light appeared at the top of the drawn blind.

Gradually Bert tilted the mirror downward. The bright spot also moved downward on the blind until it disappeared through the hole he had cut out with his knife.

The beam of reflected sunlight was now shining straight toward the tower!

Freddie and Flossie hadn't known that the Eiffel Tower was almost like a separate community or section of the city in itself. It had shops and restaurants and even a museum, not to mention a TV transmitter and a radio station up in its topmost tower.

Odile told them that when it was first built, long ago, for a world's fair in Paris, many people considered it an ugly eyesore. But in time it became the world's most

famous landmark, visited by millions of people every year.

Stepping off the elevator on the third level, they hurried to look out over the city.

"Wow! What a view!" said Freddie. All of Paris seemed spread out below them. They could see the Seine River and its bridges, the Arch of Triumph and the broad avenues, the Louvre and all the other famous buildings, Notre Dame standing on its island and the great wooded parks on the outskirts of the city . . .

Suddenly Flossie gasped. "Look, Freddie!"

"Look at what?"

"Those flashes of light!"

Some were short and some were long. Freddie began counting them. *Dot-dot-dot, dash-dash-dash, dot-dot-dot* . . . then the same pattern repeated itself, over and over again.

"Hey, those are S.O.S. signals!" the boy exclaimed. "Somebody's calling for help!"

. 10 .

The Telltale Window

The younger twins stared at each other breathlessly. "Do you s'pose it could be Bert and Nan?!" Flossie murmured.

"I dunno . . . maybe. . . . They sure knew we'd be coming up here in the Eiffel Tower after lunch!"

Just saying the words out loud seemed to convince Freddie that their hunch was right. He turned abruptly and rushed over to Odile and André. The couple were standing by themselves, holding hands and smiling at each other as they chatted.

"Somebody's calling for help!" Freddie

exclaimed. "We think maybe it's Bert and Nan!"

"Signaling for help?" André stared blankly at the boy. "What are you talking about, *mon ami?*"

"Signaling with light flashes! In Morse code! Over that way!" Freddie pointed northeast, across the Seine. "Can't you see them? They're coming from right near that building up on the hill—the one with the big white dome!"

"He means the Sacre-Coeur," said Odile.

André looked intently, and he too saw the flashes of light. "He is right!" the sailor muttered. "Somebody is flashing S.O.S. signals!"

"With a mirror, I'll bet—just like we did back home in Lakeport!" Freddie went on.

"But what makes you think it is your brother and sister who are doing it?"

"'Cause they know we can see 'em from up here in the Eiffel Tower, and they know Flossie and I can read 'em!"

"Yes, honest, Mr. André!" Flossie herself cut in earnestly. "We were playing sun-signals the day Nan got that perfume in the mail from Miss Palmer! Oh, please—can't we go and look for them? They must be in bad trouble!"

"But we don't even know where the signals are coming from," André argued.

"From someplace right near that white building!" Freddie insisted.

"That covers a lot of ground, *mon ami*."

"Can't we at least go and look around?"

"But when we are doing that, we will no longer be able to see the sun flashes—even if you are right that it is Nan and Bert who are sending them."

"Oh, please!—please!—won't you take us there?!" Flossie begged, jumping up and down in a fever of excitement. She was no longer interested in arguing—she wanted immediate action.

In the end, André and Odile gave in to the little twins' pleas, if only to avoid a scene. Neither was at all convinced that Nan or Bert could possibly be flashing the sun signals—the idea seemed too wild and far out to be taken seriously. . . . Still, it was certainly an odd coincidence . . .

The French couple felt that the Metro would be the fastest way to reach the sending area. So they and the small Bobbseys descended from the Tower and hurried toward the nearest subway station.

Paris is actually situated in a shallow river valley, or basin, with little hills called *buttes* rising on each side. The tallest of these is the hill of Montmartre on the North or Right Bank, and the lovely white Basilica of the Sacred Heart is perched on its very top.

Montmartre was once the favorite haunt of artists, and its steep cobbled streets and stone stairways still charm visitors to Paris. But Freddie's and Flossie's minds were filled with worry for the older twins' safety as they trudged along with André and

Odile. None of them even knew exactly what he was looking for. They were just hoping for a stroke of luck.

After twenty minutes of vainly roaming about, the sailor was more and more doubtful that the little twins' hunch could possibly be right.

"Believe me, there is no way that Bert and Nan could aim their signals successfully at the Eiffel Tower," he argued. "I know because I am a signalman, I have often used blinker lights at sea. But there one can *see* the beams of light in the darkness, so it is easy to tell if your signals are aimed in the right direction. But in the daytime, you cannot see your own flashes unless they are reflected off something. So, without a telescope, Bert and Nan would have no way to be sure their . . ."

André's voice trailed off, and suddenly he exclaimed, "What an idiot I am!" He slapped his forehead, adding, "Of course there is a way!"

108

"How do you mean?" said Odile, throwing her fiancé a puzzled glance.

He pointed to a top-floor window of a nearby building. It was barred, but between the bars they could see that the window blind had a hole cut in it.

"One could use a hole cut in a window blind to aim the flashes of a mirror. Come to think of it, that particular window faces directly toward the Eiffel Tower. Also, the street is so steep that the buildings in between do not get in the way, and there is plenty of sunshine coming in at an angle, through that other window just around the corner to . . ."

André broke off as Flossie interrupted eagerly. "Maybe that *is* the window the flashes of light were coming from! Couldn't we please check and see, Mr. André?"

The sailor hesitated only a moment, then exclaimed, "Why not?"

The building, which stood on a street corner, was an old brick tenement house.

André strode toward it, and they went inside to a grimy tiled vestibule.

On one wall were a number of bells and small cards bearing the tenants' names. André rang half a dozen bells at random, until somebody inside responded with a buzz on the door lock.

André immediately pushed the door open and, going through, headed up a flight of stairs. The others followed.

"André! What are you going to do?!" Odile inquired timidly, tugging her boyfriend's sleeve.

He answered with a volley of French, which seemed to mean *Don't ask me—just play it by ear, I guess!*

On the third floor, he went to the righthand front apartment and knocked. The door was opened by a tough-looking baldheaded man, who kept one hand in his suitcoat pocket.

At the sight of him, the little twins went bug-eyed with excitement. "That's the guy we saw on the bridge!" cried Freddie. "The one who tried to grab the red-haired lady's purse!"

André had already recognized him, and Baldy knew the game was up. His hand jerked upward, out of his pocket. It was clutching some kind of weapon, but André didn't wait to see what it was.

The husky young sailor hurled himself at the crook, grabbing his right arm and aiming a punch at his jaw. The bald man went reeling backward and would have toppled over if he hadn't grabbed a chair for support.

The next moment the two were fighting like madmen, punching, kicking, and swinging chairs or anything else they could lay their hands on.

But the fight didn't last long. Odile was screaming, and doors were opening along the hall. In a few minutes two caped policemen arrived and took charge.

Repeated knocks were coming from an inner doorway of Baldy's apartment and voices could be heard from within.

"I think our big sister and brother are locked in that room!" Flossie told the officers.

· 11 ·

Lady Sleuth

Seconds later, Nan and Bert were free. They hugged, and were hugged by, Flossie, Freddie and Odile. André, though somewhat bruised and battered, looked on with a happy smile.

"That was smart thinking, *mes amis*, flashing those S.O.S. signals!" he congratulated the big twins.

"*Mais oui!* And also smart of these two to read the signals!" said Odile, with her arms around Freddie and Flossie.

Meanwhile, the baldheaded crook had been handcuffed by the cops.

"He knows where our friend, Miss Palmer, is!" Nan said angrily. "I'm sure she's being held prisoner somewhere, too!"

Odile translated the conversation that followed between the two officers and the crook, so the twins would understand what was happening.

"Well, tough guy," one policeman said, "would you rather talk to us now, or wait till you get sent up for a good long stretch in prison and *then* try to make a deal, when it's too late?"

Baldy squirmed sullenly at first, but ended by spouting a full confession. "Why should I take the rap?" he grumbled. "This whole caper wasn't my idea. I was just taking orders from a rich dame who calls herself Madame Mimi."

He explained that Mimi was worried about the new perfume, *Fleur de Reve*, that Julie had created. Although it was similar to the one her own firm was about to produce, Julie's fragrance was much more appealing,

114

and Madame Mimi feared that it might ruin the sale of her own company's product. If she could get hold of a sample of *Fleur de Reve*, however, and analyze it to learn Julie's formula, she could sell it as her own creation.

Then a crook named Lachine had entered the picture.

("That's the airport thief," put in Bert, "The guy with the bushy mustache.")

Lachine had stolen the perfume from Julie's lab and was trying to sell it to the highest bidder. The price he demanded was no less than half a million francs.

Madame Mimi was furious and refused to pay him such a sum. So she had hired Baldy to steal the perfume from Lachine.

But his orders had been changed that very morning, after Madame Mimi's interview with Nan and Bert, when she learned that Julie had sent the Bobbsey girl a sample of *Fleur de Reve*.

Kidnapping the twins and demanding

115

the perfume sample as ransom had seemed like an easier, cheaper way than paying off Lachine. But her scheme had failed, thanks to the S.O.S. sun signals.

The prisoner was taken to Police Headquarters on the Ile de la Cité. The four Bobbsey twins were also driven there in a separate police car in order to tell their story firsthand and answer any questions that might help the French detectives to track down the still missing young American *parfumeuse*, Julie Palmer.

Meanwhile, Odile phoned her Aunt Colette and was soon able to talk to Mr. and Mrs. Bobbsey. They had been frantic with worry, and in constant touch with the police. Mrs. Bobbsey sobbed with relief on learning that Nan and Bert had been safely rescued.

At Police Headquarters, the twins waited for a while in an outer office. Then they were introduced to Chief Inspector Gerard, who had been put in charge of the case.

"Actually," he told the twins, "we were hunting for Lachine even before you arrived in Paris."

"How come?" Bert asked.

Chief Inspector Gerard chuckled as he stoked his pipe. "I believe, *mon fils,* that the proper person to answer that question is the detective who has spent the most time trying to collar this fellow Lachine."

He pressed a button on his desk. A moment later, the door opened and he gestured to a young woman who walked into his office.

"Allow me to present Detective Suzanne Moreau!"

The Bobbsey twins stared at her in surprise. She was the red-haired woman they had seen at the airport, on the bridge, and outside the Cathedral of Notre Dame!

. 12 .

Rescue Raid

The redhead smiled at the four American youngsters. "I am sorry I have not been able to explain things to you sooner," she apologized, "but you see, up until now I have been working undercover."

"Hey!" Freddie exclaimed suddenly, "I saved your purse after it fell in the river. We have it at our hotel."

"Shh! Don't interrupt the lady!" Nan scolded her little brother.

"Not at all," said Detective Moreau, beaming at the curly-haired little boy. "I am happy to hear such good news, and I shall see that you are rewarded for your brave work, *mon ami.* However, let me continue telling you about this case I have been working on . . ."

She explained that, after stealing Julie's perfume, Lachine had not only tried to sell it to Madame Mimi. He had also offered it to Philippe St. Yves' fashion house, because he had learned that both firms had shown interest in *Fleur de Reve.*

"Did Mr. St. Yves want to buy it, too?" Nan asked.

"*Mais non!* Unlike Madame Mimi, who is now under arrest, he immediately got in touch with us and reported Lachine's offer."

Monsieur St. Yves had then been instructed to pretend he was willing to consider a deal with the crook. And Detective Moreau was assigned to pose as his go-between and discuss the price St. Yves might be willing to pay for *Fleur de Reve.*

"That was why I met Lachine at Notre Dame," she explained, "after he sent me that gargoyle drawing to let me know the time and place for our meeting. He was extremely suspicious and wary of being caught, you see, so he wanted to take no chance that someone else might intercept the message and set a trap for him."

In order to convict Lachine, the red-haired detective went on, it was necessary to find proof of his guilt—in other words, to arrest him with the stolen perfume in his possession. But the crook was so cagey that the night before he had eluded police surveillance and shaken off the detectives who were shadowing him.

Bert frowned in surprise. "You mean you have no idea where to find him?"

Detective Moreau nodded. "To be honest, we haven't a single clue to his whereabouts. Our only hope is that he may call M'sieu St. Yves again and agree to sell him the perfume. Otherwise we have no chance of rescuing Julie Palmer—assuming that Lachine is the person who kidnapped her."

There was a grim silence in the chief inspector's office.

Suddenly Freddie popped up from his chair. "Wait a minute, Miss Moreau! Maybe I have a clue!"

"A clue?" The red-haired detective eyed him uncertainly. "What sort of clue?"

"This coin." Freddie pulled it out of his pocket to show her. "I found it in Miss Palmer's lab near her safe. That's where the perfume was stolen from."

"Our friend, the sailor, says it's an Algerian coin," Bert put in. "He's seen one like it before, in North Africa."

"*Algerian!*" Detective Moreau's face brightened and, in her eagerness, she almost snatched the coin out of Freddie's hand. "*Mon cher*, this may be the very clue we need to catch Lachine!"

"How come?" asked Flossie.

"Lachine sometimes works with an Algerian crook named Pepe Hamoud. If he is the one who dropped the coin, it may mean that he helped Lachine steal Julie Palmer's perfume—and if so, he may also have helped to kidnap her."

"Have you any idea where to find this Pepe Hamoud?" said Nan, glancing from one police officer to the other.

Chief Inspector Gerard nodded between puffs on his pipe. "Hamoud has a police record. He was arrested just two months ago for a petty street crime, but we did not have enough evidence to convict him. His dossier will show where he was living at that time, and if he is still there"— Gerard slapped his desk hard—"we will haul him in for questioning tonight!"

He picked up a telephone and gave an order. In a few moments, a police clerk brought in the file on Hamoud. His last address was on a street that Detective Moreau said was in an Arab section of Paris.

"I know this place," she told the chief

inspector, pointing to the address in Hamoud's file. "The whole building is a rabbit warren of criminals just like Hamoud himself. It would be a perfect place to hold a kidnap victim prisoner without fear of some nosy neighbor tipping off the police!"

"In that case," the chief inspector decided, "we had better take a full strike squad and surround the building."

"Ooh, boy! Can I go along too?" Freddie exclaimed.

Gerard grinned and squinted thoughtfully for a moment while scratching his jaw. "Why not, *mon fils,*" he said at last. "After all, it was your clue that may help us crack this case!"

As it turned out, all four of the Bobbsey twins were allowed to witness the raid.

Soon after nightfall, they climbed aboard what looked like a grimy, beat-up delivery van. Actually it was armor-plated and equipped with all sorts of surveillance gear, including infra-red snooperscopes, television camera and monitors, radar, radio direction finders and electronic eavesdropping devices.

Leaving Police Headquarters, it sped northeast into a slummy neighborhood, chiefly inhabited by new immigrants from North Africa and the Middle East.

The van finally pulled up across the street from the building where Pepe Hamoud lived. The driver, who was dressed in a T-shirt and work pants, opened a brown paper bag and pretended to start eating his supper.

Other cars arrived, and the police closed in from several directions. Chief Inspector Gerard, who was in the van with the twins, spoke into a microphone and gave the order to proceed.

The Bobbseys, who sat glued to TV monitors, could see everything that happened outside. They were half expecting to hear shots and explosions and the sort of loud action seen in police chase movies.

There was, in fact, some loud noise and

angry shouting, and one man tried to escape arrest by jumping out of a window. But the tough French cops soon emerged without a single shot being fired. They brought out half a dozen handcuffed prisoners, including Lachine and Hamoud—and much more importantly, an attractive but somewhat pale and haggard young woman.

"It's Julie!" Nan cried joyfully. She could hardly wait to jump out of the police van and greet her friend with a hug.

Later, at Police Headquarters, Miss Palmer told her story. A week ago, she related, after learning that two companies were interested in buying her perfume, Lachine had tried unsuccessfully to steal the formula.

Fearing another attempt, Julie pretended she was going away on a trip, hoping to mislead the unknown thief. But Lachine, with Hamoud's help, had cracked the safe in her lab, snatched the flask of perfume, and kidnapped Julie herself, intending to hold her prisoner until he suc-

125

ceeded in selling her *Fleur de Reve* fragrance to some crooked perfume company.

"Why did Lachine try to snatch Nan's bottle of perfume at the airport?" Bert asked.

"Once I knew that thieves were after my creation," Julie replied, "I wanted to make sure I had a sample of *Fleur de Reve* on hand to show the various perfume companies, just in case the next robbery attempt succeeded. It would have taken me at least two weeks, you see, to make up a new supply of the fragrance. Unfortunately, Lachine had bugged the phone at my lab, and that's how he knew about my call to Nan . . . I mean, the one that Flossie and Freddie answered."

Next day, Julie phoned Nan at the Bobbseys' hotel. "I wanted you to be the first one to hear the good news, Nan dear!" she said.

"Tell me quick!" Nan responded excitedly.

"I've just made a deal with Philippe St. Yves for his fashion house to market my *Fleur de Reve*. And when the contract is signed next Friday, I'm to receive a *huge* down payment—more money than I ever dreamed of having! And you know what's the first thing I intend to do with it?"

"I give up," said Nan as Flossie pressed her ear to the phone in order to listen in on the conversation.

"Treat you Bobbseys to a vacation on the French Riviera that you'll never forget!"